ONE IN FOUR ARE BIRDS

To Tammy at
number 8,

Thanks for reading
my book,

Best wishes,

Fiona at number 4
xxx

ONE IN FOUR ARE BIRDS

Fiona Cavell

The Book Guild Ltd

First published in Great Britain in 2019 by
The Book Guild Ltd
9 Priory Business Park
Wistow Road, Kibworth
Leicestershire, LE8 0RX
Freephone: 0800 999 2982
www.bookguild.co.uk
Email: info@bookguild.co.uk
Twitter: @bookguild

Typeset in Adobe Garamond Pro

Printed and bound in the UK by TJ International, Padstow, Cornwall

ISBN 978 1912881 253

British Library Cataloguing in Publication Data.
A catalogue record for this book is available from the British Library.

STATISTICALLY ONE IN FOUR WOMEN ARE
ABUSED AT SOME POINT IN THEIR LIVES.

CHAPTER ONE

Fiona always felt she was different from the other girls in her village. All they wanted was to settle down with an ordinary boy. Fiona was fiercely independent with no intention of settling for the ordinary, or settling down at all, so it was hard to believe that she would become preyed upon by an intimate terrorist. It was difficult to imagine that she would become trapped by someone who abused, humiliated and belittled her. She did not foresee that he would be able to take away every inch of her confidence and destroy her dignity. The other girls in the village dreamt of having their own hut to live in, like their parents had. Fiona's dream of living somewhere different unexpectedly turned into a living nightmare, from which she longed to escape, wishing she could go back to live in her parents' hut.

Fiona's village contained many pretty huts with yellow straw roofs and brightly coloured doors, and the people who lived in them were happy going about their everyday tasks. No one appeared to want to travel, to explore new ways or ideas, to go on adventures. Occasionally a villager married someone from a nearby village and moved there. That was the most exciting event that ever happened in her village. The whole village would prepare to mourn the loss of one of its residents and the departing villager would feel a terrible sadness that they were leaving the secure home that they had felt safe in and had known all their life.

Fiona had been to three other nearby villages during her childhood and found them to be remarkably similar to her own: same straw roofs, same coloured doors, same sort of villagers. She couldn't see what all the fuss was about.

Fiona longed for something different. She dreamt of meeting someone extraordinary, someone unusual. She did not wish to marry any of the boys from her village or the neighbouring ones. Even the attractive ones she found tiresome and she felt she had nothing worth saying to them, or anyone for that matter. No one appeared interesting and the conversations were always the same.

"How is your mother?"

"How is your sister?"

"How is the weather?"

"How are the animals?"

These were pointless conversations and the answers to them were already known anyway. Fiona lost her enthusiasm for talking to anyone. She became listless. She preferred to spend her time with the village animals and, as she grew up, looking after them became her full-time job.

Each villager had their own occupation so that the village functioned smoothly, and the villagers traded their skills. Some built the huts, some repaired the huts, some found the food, some cooked the food, some fed the food to those who were unable to feed themselves. Food and shelter were the most important jobs in the village. Marriage and family developed, strengthened and held the village together.

Although Fiona still lived in her parents' hut, she at least had her independence and the ability to trade. Her parents had long since given up introducing her to suitable boys to marry. The village elders would not allow a villager to occupy a hut by themselves; they were family huts. Fiona's life had remained the same since she was a child. She spent less and less time in the hut and preferred to be outside with the animals. She did not have to engage in stupid conversations with them, as an animal knows instinctively how the weather is and whether another is ill. They did not spend their time worrying about having a husband, but still were able to have young. One animal would father several young with different mothers and no one denied them shelter or banished them from the village. Fiona wondered why animals were allowed to be different.

The animals were kept within the parameters of the village, but occasionally one would stray into the forest. Fiona loved it when an inquisitive animal did this as it gave her an excuse to leave the village and feel free within the forest. The trees were not orderly like her village was. Their branches stretched and grew towards the light, bending and twisting over the years. The leaves danced and floated with the wind, falling and growing again with the seasons. The flowers were not planted in neat rows but sprung up wherever they pleased. The weeds teased the trees edging onto their territory without fear of reciprocation, creeping and surrounding and capturing whatever space they wanted. The wild animals knew no boundaries and darted and roamed around the forest. The birds flew free.

No animal had to wear clothes. The villagers were not allowed to roam around naked and wore the skins of dead animals. Fiona used to wonder why she had to look like one of the animals but not behave like one. She questioned the rules but was told by her mother that the people who made them were wise and she should not question but follow them.

At the beginning of the forest just outside the village, a woman lived alone. She didn't follow the rules of the village but lived off the forest. She only occasionally traded with the villagers if there was something she could not get from the forest, but she found the earth supplied her with most things. If she needed to trade, she would offer the villagers one of the beautiful crafts she had made out of vines or wood from the trees. These crafts were exquisite and were often presented to villagers upon marriage or the celebration of the birth of a child. The villagers thought her a witch or a madwoman for not conforming, but Fiona thought her wise. In fact, she thought she would one day take on that role as she longed not to be like the rest of the villagers. The wise woman was called Maggie, and Fiona had never heard her speak. As Fiona passed her in the forest while looking for a wandering animal, Maggie would smile, or wave and Fiona would smile back. Maggie was beautiful, with long hair turning grey in the autumn of her life and kind, wise eyes. Her hut didn't have a brightly coloured door but was the natural colour of the forest. It didn't have perfect symmetry, but instead bulged and spread unequally as Maggie had clearly built and repaired it herself as she seldom traded her skills with the villagers.

In the past Fiona had learned that Maggie had traded by teaching the village children but had left the village when the elders had found her teachings too unorthodox. Fiona had asked her parents what it was that Maggie had taught that the elders didn't like, and her mother had told her the conflict was mainly about Maggie telling the young girls they didn't need a husband, and clearly they did, because that was the village way of life.

Fiona had heard this story from her mother when she was a young girl and had been fascinated by it. "Why do we have to marry?" she would ask.

Her mother's reply was always "Because it is our way; you cannot live alone."

"But Maggie does!" Fiona would insist, and jump up and down, questioning everything she was told, but soon after she was told to be quiet.

In the end Fiona did become quiet and found no one she wanted to marry. She knew she was a disappointment and already labelled as different. She knew her parents were ashamed of her, and one day she would inevitably have to leave the village and live alone off the forest in a sad-looking bulging hut.

Then one day Fiona's life changed. A dark stranger turned up in the village, quite unlike anyone she had ever met before. He stood tall and proud with a long neck and enormous shoulders. His beady eyes were jet black, darting around, quickly surveying his surroundings, until they rested on Fiona's face and smiled. The stranger was welcomed into the village by the elders, Peter and Michael, who offered him a guest hut and a feast, as was their tradition. The villagers gathered around and brought the finest food, and they ate together and listened to the stranger's tales.

The stranger called himself Sicarus, and claimed he lived in a village far away, beyond the forest, where people lived not in huts with straw roofs, but in houses high up in the trees, made of sticks. Fiona sat, fascinated to hear of new and exciting places beyond her imagination; her pulse raced, and her eyes opened wide, fixed on the stranger.

After the villagers departed for their huts, Fiona's parents signalled to her to leave too and let the stranger be. But she couldn't. She was mesmerised. "I will be home soon." She waved, lingering, hoping Sicarus would accept her company. And he did.

They talked half the night, and Sicarus lavished Fiona with his attention. He told her stories of his adventures in faraway places and filled her mind with new and exciting ideas. Her face was illuminated in the moonlight, and for the first time in her life she really adored being with someone, and longed to remain with him. She finally realised that she had the potential to no longer want to be alone and could fit in with the village values after all. Perhaps her parents and the rest of the village were right; this was the way things were meant to be and she could live happily with a man. All her life she had been waiting for this moment and now it was upon her. She enjoyed talking to him so much that they sat together and talked all night until the moon yawned and closed his weary eyes.

As dawn drew nearer Sicarus asked Fiona if she wanted to see something truly wonderful, but she must promise to keep what he was to show her a secret. Fiona promised, and was told by Sicarus to creep away with him, so no one could see. Her heart beat faster and Fiona was shocked as Sicarus whispered to her, "I can fly." At the sight of her puzzled face, he told her that he had developed a special power whereby he could turn into a bird for a little while and fly into the sky. "During that time, I will be unable to speak, so you must listen now to my instructions to keep yourself safe and do exactly as I tell you."

Fiona nodded, unable to comprehend the situation, wondering if she could be dreaming.

"Stay away from me whilst I am transforming," Sicarus commanded, "or you may get scratched. When I am done, I will nod my head and you must climb onto my back and place both arms around my neck and hold on tight. Do not under any circumstances obstruct my wings. Now stand very still over there."

Fiona moved aside and stood exactly where she was told, trembling while the transformation started. She saw Sicarus start to extend his beautiful long neck and raise his arms, his powerful shoulders expanding as spikes began to break through his skin. He began to screech, apparently in pain, which made Fiona startle and want to run away but she stood firm, against her instincts. The spikes grew bigger and began to unfold and fan out into feathers and started to cover his body. Soon his skin was no longer visible, and all Fiona could see were sleek black feathers. His body shape changed from slim and upright to puffed and angular, the base of his spine spreading out into a feathery array. His legs became thinner and scaly, and his feet stretched out into three sharp claws rooting into the ground.

Within a few moments his face gave way to that of a bird, a black beak protruding from his features which were now unrecognisable except for those beady black eyes. Fiona was terrified, but when the bird nodded his head, she did exactly what she had been told and climbed onto his soft, feathered back and placed her arms around his ruffled neck, being careful not to touch his wings.

Her fear soon turned to exhilaration as he took off and started to fly above her village until the huts were tiny dots below. They flew towards the shining stars, the cool moon whispering through her hair that she was the only girl he had ever seen flying past him. The moon was fully awake again, excited by the night's events, keeping the dawn waiting patiently until she could awake the earth. Fiona felt special, privileged, a stranger in a part of the universe which belonged only to magical creatures. They soared over other villages, their tiny lights like pinpricks, dark, eerie forests and majestic mountains rising proudly in the moonlight.

Fiona didn't want her adventure to end, but eventually the bird circled and swooped down towards her village, landing smoothly on the ground, his sharp claws digging into the earth. She climbed carefully off his back, expecting the bird to transform back into Sicarus, but he flew away in silence. She stood there for a while, wondering if he would come back, but no one came. Fiona didn't know what to do. She had just experienced the best and most wonderful time of her life, but now she stood there, all alone again and cold. Her mind was telling her that nothing that had just happened was real, but her heart was telling her she had just met the man of her childhood dreams. But never had she dreamt of a man with magical powers. This was beyond anything her imagination could have created. The man she had met was interesting, attractive, unimaginably magical and irresistible. But why had he left her? Couldn't he have turned back into Sicarus? Was he coming back?

Then a terrible thought struck her: was she unattractive to him? Had she done something wrong whilst on his back? Would she ever see him again?

Deep panic set in. She had never felt such insecurity before. Perhaps he had taken many girls flying and then left them. But then she remembered the moon so coolly whispering to her that she was the only one he had seen. Her head began to spin, and suddenly it all became too much for her brain to process. She needed sleep, so eventually she drifted back to her family's hut and fell asleep as the dawn finally let herself in.

CHAPTER TWO

The following morning Fiona awoke to Sicarus and nearly half of the village crowded into her hut, surrounding her. She must have been so tired that she had slept through them all coming in. Her mum was beaming.

"It's all sorted," she announced proudly. "You can have the wedding here next week. Unfortunately, Sicarus' parents live far away so they won't be able to make it."

Fiona sat bolt upright in shock. Wedding? Her head whirled as the faces of the villagers' span past, all smiling. Sicarus had come back! He was real! He did want her! He wanted to marry her! But he hadn't asked her, and she had only met him the day before. Next week? Everyone seemed so happy, and Sicarus had clearly planned it all with her parents without her knowledge or consent. What should she say? What should she do? But of course, she would consent. Why wouldn't she? He was the man of her dreams and the best man she had ever met in her life. Everything was just happening so fast. Then Fiona started to smile, especially when she saw her parents' proud faces. She was no longer at risk of becoming the outsider, the madwoman in a bulging, uneven hut.

The villagers prepared for the wedding, weaving brightly coloured flowers around where the ceremony would be and preparing the food. Sicarus remained in the village for the week, but the couple snuck off most nights to fly around the sky. It had been the best week of Fiona's life. She was enjoying the romance, their special secret. She was also enjoying her parents' attention. She found she could have conversations with them again, and with the other villagers. "How are the preparations coming along?" the villagers would ask her, and she would ask of them. Both sides knew the answer to the question as it was obvious from the state of the village, but this time Fiona did not see it as a pointless question. Now she was truly conversing with the villagers and had a common theme with them at long last. And every night she looked forward to her magical flight past the moon.

Each night Sicarus transformed into the bird, and she stood where he told her to and did exactly what he said. How kind he was, wanting to keep her safe during the transformation and the flight, she thought as she looked at his sharp talons one night. The moon whispered to her every night that she was still the only girl he had ever seen flying by. The thrill of the flight, the coldness of the night air, the magical night sky all continued to take her breath away. Never in her wildest dreams had she imagined such an adventure. She looked forward with excitement to her imminent marriage to this magical stranger, to a life ahead that was better than she could have ever imagined.

She knew now why she hadn't wanted to marry any of the village boys. She was clearly destined for something more special.

Each night he transformed into the bird, but unlike the first night, after the flight he changed back into Sicarus and did not leave her. On one night the flight seemed much longer than the previous ones, and eventually they set down in a dark, thick, unknown forest. The bird beckoned Fiona to get down and changed back into Sicarus again, his feathers folding in on themselves, turning into spikes and disappearing to reveal his skin, his beak shrinking away to form a smiling mouth once more.

"I want you to meet my parents," Sicarus said solemnly, "but don't be shocked; they are not like me. They enjoy using their powers and may be birds when you meet them as they like to test things." He told her they would not come to the wedding out of principle, as they liked being birds whereas he preferred his human form. He hoped she would understand and respect their wishes and be polite and not make a scene. He then led her to a clearing, where she was shocked indeed.

Two large black birds were fighting over a giant worm. They were squawking and digging their talons into the ground, uprooting the earth, sending soil and stones flying. A stone hit Fiona hard on the leg, making her cry out. This caused the birds to turn around to look at her and momentarily drop the huge worm. The worm was only half alive, battered and covered in blood, squirming and wriggling slowly, attempting to find a way underground, away from its predators. Fiona gasped upon seeing the birds' faces, their greedy beaks splattered with blood and chunks of flesh, their beady black eyes reflecting their murderous souls. They squawked and looked away from Fiona and Sicarus, pecking again at their target, the dying worm, and finally ripping it savagely into smithereens, blood oozing into the earth.

Sicarus told Fiona she should be polite and introduce herself. She was, after all, to be their daughter-in-law. Fiona choked back her tears and tried to retain her good manners, claiming she was pleased to meet them, and she would make Sicarus happy when they married.

The large black birds ignored her, still covered in blood, and squawked to their son, "What about Guinness?"

Sicarus bowed to them and nodded. He later explained that they were having trouble accepting Fiona as his future wife and had wanted him to marry his last girlfriend, called Guinness, as she was one of them. That was all Fiona's future parents-in-law could say. They wouldn't acknowledge her, try and be polite, or even look at her. She wasn't good enough in their eyes; their black, beady, murderous eyes.

Sicarus led Fiona silently away, sobbing in disbelief. He transformed without a word and she climbed on his back, her leg still stinging from the stone. On the journey home she tried to concentrate on the beauty of the stars and breathe the still night air. She could not understand how someone as beautiful and magical as Sicarus could have come from those horrible creatures. It made no sense, so all she could do was forget it and put it down to a freak of nature; after all, Sicarus had already told her he was not like them, and how honest he was in showing her his terrible embarrassment, revealing all to her as he must love her so much.

The wedding was to be the following day, and when they returned to her village Fiona spent the night with Sicarus, allowing him to bathe her bruised leg with soothing tenderness, taking control of her every need. She had never spent the night with him before and was worried that she wouldn't know what to do, or he might do something she didn't like, but the experience was perfect, peaceful, seductive, smooth, but also exciting, stimulating and revitalising. She realised now why women wanted to marry; it was the most natural, normal thing in the world, an inevitable consequence of life. She could hardly remember why she hadn't wanted it before, why she'd felt she would rather be alone. Her body felt complete now, she had finally grown up and become part of nature, even if it was with a magical and almost unnatural person. She cuddled up to his mystical body, pondering these things until she finally fell into a peaceful sleep.

The wedding was beautiful, and Fiona felt proud to be with such a handsome, exceptional stranger. She forgot all about the horror of his parents, the worm they tortured and how they had ignored her. She was just happy he had chosen her and not his last girlfriend to be his wife. She felt privileged.

After the wedding feast, Sicarus announced that Fiona would be living with him in his house made of sticks high above the treetops, and she would have everything there she needed; all she had to do was ask. Although Fiona had accepted that on her marriage, she would leave her parents' hut, she hadn't actually thought about giving up her occupation of looking after the village animals, losing the ability to trade in her own right, and her independence. She had assumed that they would be given a hut in the village that Sicarus had now become a part of. A village that had made her feel safe all her life. She did not really want to leave her parents, especially now they had become proud of her for finally finding someone to marry. She did not want to leave her animals either.

Still, she had chosen Sicarus now and she was happy that she would have the type of life she had always dreamt of, living in a faraway place with someone adventurous. So she said goodbye to her parents, the villagers and her animals, whom Sicarus had arranged to be looked after by her mother, and left hand in hand with her new husband.

"Don't forget to come back and visit." Her mother smiled behind tears of joy to see her daughter's dream come true. Fiona also had tears, but they were of sadness for leaving the village, and the villagers mourned Fiona's departure.

CHAPTER THREE

As soon as the village was behind them, Sicarus transformed into a bird once more and they soared high above the trees and landed in a little house made of sticks, isolated high up in one of the tallest trees. As Sicarus transformed back into himself once more, Fiona couldn't help but be impressed with the house which was now her home. It was comfortable and spacious with spectacular views of the whole forest. For a while she was happy with Sicarus in her treetop home. Occasionally he would transform into the bird and they would set off on adventures together, or he would go alone and bring her back beautiful presents of exotic fruits or flowers. Her life was complete, and happily she discovered she was having a baby, and nothing pleased her more than to think they would be their own little family. Again, she smiled to herself, thinking how wrong she had been not believing, a few months earlier, that she would ever be married.

She did still miss her parents and her animals and wondered how they were. Whenever she suggested to

Sicarus that they should go back to visit he always came up with other, lovelier things to do: a flight to see the cool blue ocean or the snow-capped mountains.

Before their first baby was born, they had a beautiful flight beneath the stars. Just as Fiona was trying to climb off the bird, she lost her centre of gravity. Her belly had become heavier and as she fell, she reached out and grabbed hold of the bird's wing. Immediately the bird reacted and threw Fiona off, stamping on her belly with his talons and scratching her chest. He then squawked off, leaving Fiona in a bloodied huddle. She was shocked and hurt. How could her beloved Sicarus have done that to her and, even worse, their unborn child? She broke down and cried. She had never felt so scared and alone.

A few minutes later Sicarus returned full of remorse, reminding Fiona she had promised never to touch his wings, and this was the consequence which she had brought upon herself. Fiona wept bitterly both for herself and her unborn baby but felt guilty that perhaps she was responsible for what had happened as Sicarus suggested. He told her repeatedly that she was to blame for his actions, and even became cross at her for hurting their baby as a result. He demanded an apology, which Fiona freely gave, still in a state of shock. He warned her again never to touch his wings as he could not control his reaction when under pressure. They were his magical wings which had given Fiona everything, and she needed to respect them. Fiona was full of remorse.

Following this incident, Sicarus refused to let Fiona fly again while she was pregnant. "You will probably spoil it again and grab on to my wing," he said firmly. "I don't want you causing me any further difficulties." Fiona begged to let them fly again, but he cast her aside and told her she was selfish and there would be no more flying until he could trust her to do as she was told. She begged and begged, but nothing would change his ruling. Fiona finally gave up and bitterly regretted her actions. Without the flying she felt trapped above the treetops, and she wanted more than ever to visit her parents but Sicarus would not allow her to leave.

Fiona felt imprisoned. For the first time since she had been there, she realised she could not leave the house unless he took her. She was scared. "What if you have an accident one day and I am unable to get out?" she tried to reason with him. "What if we are struck by lightning while you are away?" Sicarus told her nothing like that would ever happen, but she began to fear more. Deep panic set in. If she tried to reason with him he wouldn't listen. If she begged him, he wouldn't listen. If she cried, he wouldn't listen. So, she had to try a new tactic: give him what he wanted so that he might just listen to her.

"What can I do for you to make you happier?" she asked him softly, choking back her tears. "So that you will trust me and let me have an emergency escape route to come and find you to help you if you are hurt and unable to fly?" She suggested a simple rope or ladder so that she could climb down to the forest floor and promised not to use it other than to help him should he ever become injured and unable to fly. "I would do anything for you," she vowed as he smiled selfishly.

"As you want me to make you this rope ladder, there is something you can do for me if you are serious about doing anything for me." He grinned. "It's a tiny favour compared to what you are asking of me," he continued, his grin widening.

"Anything," Fiona promised. "Please let me have the opportunity to do what you want." Her heart sunk inside her chest as she knew she had sunk lower than she ever would have wanted. She had compromised herself, like she had always promised to herself from a young age she would never do for anyone, let alone a man. She knew what he would ask. And here she was begging him, like one of the girls from the village she had always said she didn't want to be like. Going against her instincts and her own sense of worth to please her husband in the hope he would do something for her. Sacrificing herself for his ugly, selfish pleasures and begging him for the opportunity.

"All right then." He finally gave in to her begging, grabbed the top of her head and forced her to her knees. "If you insist."

Fiona tried not to vomit by swallowing hard and breathing slowly. She hoped it would be over soon. Sicarus clearly enjoyed every minute and did his best to make it last for as long as possible. Fiona got the impression that the more upset she was and disliked what was happening, the happier Sicarus became. He became most excited by her dread, torment and fear. Realising how he appeared to gain energy from her pain was difficult for her to process, but her own survival mode took over and she learned to pretend she enjoyed doing such a disgusting act. This was the only way, it seemed, to lessen his depraved gratification in hurting her. To get through what she had agreed to do, simply to move on to the next day.

A few weeks later they had a beautiful daughter they named Gabrielle. Sicarus was a devoted father, seeing to Fiona and Gabrielle's every need, although Fiona was still essentially unable to go out. The tree house now had a rope ladder leading to the ground, but it was dangerous enough for one person to climb down, let alone with a babe in arms. But the baby brought her a new lease of life and Fiona was even happier with her new family. The baby was quite demanding, though, and required Fiona's constant attention, and one day an unexpected thing happened.

While Gabrielle was crying, and Fiona was trying hopelessly to calm her, Sicarus suddenly started shouting and pacing the tree house faster and faster, and then his feet transformed into talons and he turned into the bird. Not because he intended to fly them on a stargazing flight around the yellow moon to soothe the baby, but because, it appeared, his anger and impatience had simply transformed him.

Fiona held her breath, and somehow the baby sensed her fear and stopped crying. All was silent as the bird looked at her with his beady black eyes and started to peck at her. Fiona was holding the baby in her arms, and so all she could do was to hold her tightly to her chest and let herself be pecked and scratched by the bird's talons. The horrible hard beak stabbed her skin several times, hammering into her with thudding pain; the talons were sharp knives piercing her skin with burning pain. The pain was so intense and unexpected she was in shock and simply froze, allowing the bird to hurt her as much as he desired.

The bird then flew away. Fiona was left bleeding. Her flesh was torn, and huge purple bruises started to form beneath her skin. She felt lifeless, abandoned and unable to understand what had just happened. Sicarus had attacked her on purpose because he was angry. He had transformed into the bird without magic or wonder, but out of hatred and apparently involuntarily. Fiona had always believed this magical transformation was something he could stop and start whenever he wanted to bring them joy, but she did not feel joy now; she felt in danger.

Tears streamed down her face. How could he let the bird take over him out of anger and attack her? Worse still, how could he attack her with their baby in her arms? What if he had hurt the baby? She looked down at Gabrielle, still in her arms. She looked just like an angel, and Fiona's heart was filled with love. Then she noticed tiny red specks of blood on the baby angel's white dress; Fiona's blood had splashed her when the bird had attacked and pecked at her arms. Fiona gently tried to wipe the blood away, but the tiny dress was also wet with her tears, and the more she tried to wipe it, the more the blood mixed with the tears and they became one, larger blots of salt-watered blood absorbing into the white fabric, turning a pretty pink colour to match the angel's rosy lips. Fiona kissed those perfect lips and felt peace. She sat there, babe in arms, the baby still quiet, unable to move while her body began the process of healing itself.

A few hours later Sicarus returned, not as the bird as he usually flew into the tree house, but as a man, climbing up the rope ladder carrying a large bunch of forest flowers and delicious fruits. "I am so sorry," he said. "I can normally control when I transform; I don't know what happened. It must be because I was overtired with not sleeping because of the baby. You really need to get that baby into a better routine, so it sleeps through the night." He then went over to Gabrielle and started playing with her, making her laugh.

"Dada." She said her first word, which made Fiona beam, despite her horrific injuries. Sicarus picked up Gabrielle and changed her clothes, dressing her in a golden gown he had brought for her and throwing the bloodstained dress away without a word, and played with Gabrielle for the rest of the day.

Sicarus was kind to Fiona after that; he looked after Gabrielle while Fiona rested, allowing her injuries to fully heal. The bruises faded, and the cuts scabbed over, forming new skin underneath. While her body healed, her mind could not heal itself of the ill caused to it, keeping Fiona awake with terrifying thoughts, dreaming that Sicarus would harm her again or, worse still, harm Gabrielle. Some days Fiona watched Sicarus playing with Gabrielle and seemingly showing her love and caring for her, and she began to feel guilty that she could even dream that he might hurt his own child. Perhaps what had happened was truly a one-off, something out of the blue, and they could be a happy family again.

As Gabrielle grew, Fiona wondered whether it would be helpful for her to have a playmate, a brother or sister to have fun with and share experiences together, although deep down she did fear Sicarus' reaction to a crying baby.

But she felt Gabrielle needed this, so she went on and had another child, this time a boy she named Jegudiel. Sicarus was surprisingly agreeable to the idea of having another baby, and even boasted about his potency. However, during the pregnancy, he became unsupportive and told Fiona that because the baby was her idea, she would have to deal with the consequences. By the time she was almost due to give birth, he told her that she would have to do this alone and look after Gabrielle, as she had wanted this, not him, and he had more important things to do than look after Gabrielle at her request. Fiona bitterly regretted getting pregnant, and realised she was on her own. She begged Sicarus to help, but he tormented her and agreed only to look after Gabrielle during the birth as a favour to her, provided she would do a small favour for him. Fiona reluctantly agreed as he forced her to her knees. "What have I become?" she wept bitterly afterwards. She had become his slave.

During Jegudiel's birth Sicarus assisted Fiona and carried out his promise to look after Gabrielle. After the birth he even held his son and acted the proud father.

But whilst Jegudiel brought fun and laughter he also cried, and this once again set off an accidental transformation on Sicarus' part when he ended up annoyed by the crying baby and started pacing, pecking and scratching Fiona. This time the attack was more brutal. The bird dug his claws into Fiona's face and arms while she was trying to feed Jegudiel.

"Please don't kill our baby," she pleaded as she tried to shelter the child from his father. The beady black eyes looked back at her with no remorse, no emotion, and the scaly orange claws struck at her again, tearing at her skin, ripping it apart, bright red blood escaping from within. Fiona feared the worst, and frantic thoughts of a dying, bloodied baby filled her traumatised mind. "You will not have him!" she screamed at the bird as she hunched her shoulders, lowered her head and engulfed Jegudiel with her body so no part of him remained exposed. She knew this meant exposing herself and braced herself for excruciating pain. The bird was happy to have a target and jumped on her shoulders, clawing down her back, creating crimson tracks, marking a mother's sacrificial love. Her right shoulder was hurting beyond any pain she had previously felt, and she could feel the hot blood gushing from the cruel gash caused by one of the talons sticking into her flesh and becoming entangled in her shredded skin. Eventually the bird flew off and Fiona remained on the floor, holding baby Jegudiel for a few moments until she was able to struggle to her feet and put the sleeping baby to bed in the room he shared with his sister, who appeared to have slept through the whole attack.

The following morning Sicarus was there and saw her injuries, for which he apologised when he eventually spoke to her. He again brought presents of beautiful flowers, exotic fruits and fine clothes for the children, and was extra attentive to the family. He played with the children, making them laugh and sing, and brought healing potions to help Fiona's wounds. This time one of her wounds did not heal properly but turned into an ugly red scar across her shoulder, serving as a constant reminder of the bird's temper. Sicarus again made excuses for the bird's conduct; the second baby was, after all, Fiona's idea. She was the one who had wanted Jegudiel and had put extra pressure upon Sicarus to find them food and provide for them, let alone all the added pressure of a crying baby stopping him sleeping properly.

Fiona looked at Jegudiel, so innocent and beautiful, a gift from heaven, but now an unwanted gift that she couldn't return. "I wish you hadn't been born," she sobbed silently to herself as she gazed at the joint most precious thing in her life. Gabrielle and Jegudiel were all Fiona truly loved now. Gone was her regard for the handsome, magical stranger she had first laid eyes on a few years earlier; gone were her hopes and dreams of exciting adventures in faraway places. All she wanted was to have a hut in her village with a brightly coloured door and never go back to her treetop house made of sticks and her life of captivity.

As time passed, Fiona was alarmed to notice Sicarus' accidental transformations became more frequent; at first monthly, then more like weekly, and then almost every day. Things she wouldn't expect to set him off made him angry, such as asking him when he was going to bring food back, but on other occasions she would ask the same question and get a reasonable response. The not knowing when she would be attacked or how severe it would be caused her anxiety which was almost, but not as bad as the attacks themselves. The attacks always took the same pattern: anger, transformation into the bird, pecking, scratching, screaming, bleeding, flying away, returning as Sicarus, sometimes sorrow, sometimes blame.

But one day, the pattern changed.

CHAPTER FOUR

Fiona guessed that she had been attacked by the bird on at least forty occasions, although she had lost count. But never by Sicarus. Until one night as they lay together in the tree house. Both children were asleep, there was nothing for Sicarus to get angry over, and so this attack was the most shocking and the most brutal. He started to scratch her back with his fingernails, retracing old scars caused by the bird.

"Please, Sicarus, stop it; you are hurting me," she whispered, trying not to wake the children. But he didn't. She pleaded with him, she tried to bargain with him, she tried reasoning with him, crying, but nothing would stop him. He dug in his nails, furrowing into her skin following the lines of past attacks, drawing tracks of blood. She was too worried to scream out, partly for fear of the children waking and partly because he might turn into the bird and she was so frightened of what would happen if he did. But she later realised Sicarus was in fact as dangerous, if not more, than the bird.

She fought to stop him, trying to force his arms away from her, but he was too strong, and it made him dig in harder. She knew he was going to hurt her in the worst way possible as he started to tear at her clothes. He ripped her clothes just as the bird had torn her flesh. There was no mercy. Only his desire to find a victim and overpower her. To cause her deep fear and draw the very life out of her. To make her his and torture her body and weaken her mind. To treat her as an object of his depraved fantasy and play his sick games. Fiona thought of herself as a mouse being tossed up in the air by a cat, playing with its prey over and over, almost allowed to go free, hoping it could struggle to get away, but being caught again by its clever predator, and wooed into the dance of death.

The more she struggled, the more he seemed to enjoy hurting her, and eventually she gave up and let her exhausted body rest. Her mind was still as the attack went on and she realised she was unable to protect herself. Now she could see clearly as her mind flashed back to the horror she felt when she met his savage parents, birds devouring and destroying an innocent creature.

Sicarus was not a man who could magically transform into a bird. He was a bird who could pretend to be a man.

Suddenly it all made sense and she realised she had been fooled. How could she have been so stupid? She cursed herself for not seeing any of the warning signs. His parents were vile creatures who had made her feel sick, and yet at the time she hadn't been able to see that he was the same as them. She had been fooled into thinking he was special and that she deserved to live a life different to the others in her village. Well, she certainly had that now. With hindsight she would have been far better off marrying any one of the boring boys from her village, even one of the not-so-attractive ones, because she would have been safe. And now she wasn't safe, and neither were her children. He was attacking her and all she could do was wait until it was over and regret ever meeting him.

After the attack was over, Sicarus smiled and settled down to sleep. Fiona's mind and body felt sick and she knew she had to get away. She could never go through that again. She could never let him touch her again; she never wanted to see him again. What he had done to her was beyond horror. He had forcibly taken her body, and with it her very soul had been taken too. She had no feelings. She had nothing left. She had been violated by him. In the past she had offered him her body voluntarily, desiring him to take her, to show her love but instead he had shown her violence. Then the love had gone and been replaced with power and control. She hated him now.

She didn't want to leave the children in his care, but there was no way she could get them down the rope ladder. They would surely fall to their deaths. She shuddered, torn and heartbroken, contemplating whether it would be better if she fell to her death. Her life was unimportant now; she was just an empty shell. She wanted to die. To end the pain she was feeling. She knew it would never go away until she died. Death was the only answer, it beckoned her; she just had to jump, and the pain would end there. But she couldn't leave the children. They were her life, and she had given them life. She couldn't abandon them with no mother, no one to guide and protect them, to love them and be there for them. No one to stop the bird or Sicarus harming them.

She resolved to get away, find help, and whoever she found would help her get her children back. They would then be safe and away from the bird forever. For now, the children would have to remain sleeping. She went over to where they slept, their angelic faces shining. "I promise on my life I will be back soon, my darlings," she whispered. "I will never abandon you." She was so scared that Sicarus would find her gone and take it out on the children. Her only hope was that she had not yet seen him hurt his own children; it was only ever her.

She crept down the rope ladder, unable to see in the midnight sky. Even the moon was hiding tonight. With each step down she felt she would lose her footing and fall, but eventually she stood on the forest floor, the cruel twigs cutting into her feet as she commenced the journey back to her village. Fiona had never walked there before, although she had flown above it so she knew the route, following every familiar landmark, the hills, the riverbank, recognising familiar rocks which seemed far larger from the ground.

By sunrise she wasn't even halfway home. The children would wake soon, wondering where she was. Her heart sank. She was tired, hungry, thirsty and cold, her feet were blistered and cut, and every injury Sicarus had inflicted on her the night before throbbed and ached. But she had to carry on. Her feet hurt so much that eventually she could no longer take her own weight on them and she continued on all fours, although her hands were equally injured. She crawled through the forest, hoping each step wouldn't be her last. At times she longed to give up, to give way to the dark earth and let her body be taken for a second time.

The thought of her beautiful children was the only thing that prevented her from dying. She struggled on. The pain she felt was unbelievable, but she had no other choice. She concentrated on the angelic faces of her children to keep focused, moving hands and feet in a rhythm similar to those of the drums played at the funeral when someone died in her village.

Fiona eventually turned up at her village ripped, ragged, haggard, exhausted and completely drained. Her mother greeted her with a blanket and some water. "We have been so worried," she cried. "Sicarus is here with the children and has explained everything. We can't believe you abandoned your children like this. You must be very ill. You were very foolish trying to persuade him to have another baby; he says you are probably a few days pregnant and your hormones must have caused you to go insane."

Sicarus appeared, smiling. "My God, Fiona, what have you done to yourself? I'm so glad you have come back to us."

Fiona collapsed, and he caught her in his arms and carried her with those broad shoulders back to her parents' hut, where she slept for many hours.

CHAPTER FIVE

When she awoke Fiona tried to tell everyone that Sicarus was a bird, but no one listened. "You're delirious," her father said gravely. "You nearly lost your life, and if you are not careful you will lose your children; you must think of the unborn one. Sicarus has told us how reluctant he was when you begged him for another baby, and how he thinks you have taken on too much, but he has promised to stand by you. He is so kind."

Fiona tried to protest that she hadn't wanted another baby, hadn't wanted any of this and Sicarus had overpowered her, but Sicarus spoke over her and told everyone how crazy she had been acting lately. As soon as she was rested, they would need to get her back into her normal routine, which would no doubt ease her mental illness. He would look after her.

Outside the hut, Maggie, the wise woman who lived alone at the edge of the village, was listening. She knocked on the door and came in. "I have made you a handcrafted sling for your baby when it is born. The baby will feel close to you when you carry it around."

Fiona was surprised to hear Maggie speak but thanked her and accepted it as a gift. Maggie would have been aware that Fiona was now an outsider and had nothing to trade with her. The kindness brought tears to Fiona's eyes. Maggie then left without another word lowering her head to avoid eye contact with Sicarus.

Fiona turned to Gabrielle and Jegudiel. "Do you want us to go back to the forest with Daddy now?" Her eyes were pleading, hoping the children would sense her pain and realise their dad's true nature, but they were too young. They only saw the flying, fun Daddy, and eagerly said they wanted to return. Fiona knew she had no choice but to go back.

Fiona felt ill. She didn't want to go back to Sicarus, but what choice in real terms did she have? She couldn't have her old life back; she was married with two children and a third on the way. She believed she no longer belonged in the village but had nowhere else to live. She had no trade, no independence. She had deliberately turned her back on village life, and not surprisingly, she did not feel that she was welcome back. She had chosen Sicarus, and now she must face the consequences no matter how awful they were. She felt that she deserved this life for being so foolish in the first place by falling in love with him. She bowed her head and allowed Sicarus to take them away. Her parents waved goodbye and were pleased their daughter was not separating from her children's father as that would bring shame and conflict on the village, as it could involve decisions from a neighbouring village about occupancy of a hut or where and with whom the children should live, in accordance with the village customs.

✒

Upon their return to the house made of sticks in the treetop, Fiona felt sick. She knew the wrath of Sicarus would be upon her and he would punish her for leaving. She just didn't know when. At first, he was surprisingly nice to her, making her food and drink, playing with the children, but then after three days his anger came. Luckily the children were in bed when he turned into the bird. He pecked and scratched at her and showed no mercy. He screeched at her and dug his sharp claws into every inch of her skin. He stamped on her head, and she instinctively turned over to protect her unborn and unwanted baby. The bird then jumped on her back, and onto the very base of her spine and further down past her tail bone. To her horror he stayed there, pinning her to the floor and tearing at her clothes with his beak. The hard, persistent beak pecked deeper, burrowing into her, forcing her cheeks apart with crude and vile shrieks of pleasure as Fiona screamed in pain, unable to move for fear the bird would kill the tiny baby inside and towards the front of her. So she simply lay still and allowed the bird to attack her from behind. She could feel blood gushing from deep gashes the bird had created, running down and covering her legs, a cruel mock labour, which felt like her intestines were being ripped out.

When she could take no more, she turned over onto her bloodied back revealing her stomach, white and bare in surrender, her legs slightly open due to the horrific pain shooting though her, accepting that she had inevitably failed to protect her unborn child. She thought the bird would surely jump on her front, peck as deeply as it had on the other side and destroy the tiny baby within. But instead the bird jumped on her head again and kicked her in the face with those sharp talons, with such force it knocked her out.

When she regained consciousness, the bird had changed into Sicarus again. He told her that she had deserved punishing for leaving him and trying to turn others against him. He threatened that if she ever tried to leave him again, he would take her children and she would never see them again as he would persuade everyone that she was an unfit mother. Fiona shrunk, predicting that the villagers would obviously believe him given how everyone had reacted last time. No one had listened or believed her about the bird and she had instead come across as mad.

Just to make sure Sicarus said he would remove the rope ladder and she would never be able to leave the house. Fiona was finally trapped.

For the following months Fiona and the children were imprisoned in the house made of sticks high up in the trees. As Fiona's belly swelled with the unborn baby growing daily, she became completely under Sicarus' control. She dared not upset him and did everything he asked to try and keep him calm and prevent him from hurting the baby inside her. He still transformed into the bird often, but when he did she simply cowered in a corner, arms and legs protecting the baby. Sometimes he would fly off for days, leaving them without food so she and particularly the children were pleased to see him when he eventually returned with food and treats.

On one occasion the bird flew away for five days. Fiona had food for the children for probably two or three days at the most. On the fourth day both children cried for most of the day from hunger. Fiona did her best to comfort them, but she too was weak. On the fifth day she prayed and promised that if the bird would just return and feed the children and let them live, then he could have her life and she would gladly surrender it. But still he didn't return.

Fiona was so desperate that she scoured the bin and the floor looking for food and picked up every crumb, mouldy and unwholesome, she could find. She offered the children these dirty scraps and they took them eagerly, begging for more. It reminded her of the wild animals, who lived in the forest, and the villagers who called them dirty, scrounging scavengers. She had sunk so low since her marriage that the original Fiona from the village, who would never marry, was fiercely independent and had her own occupation and ability to trade, was unrecognisable.

As the time approached for the baby to be born, Fiona started to prepare for its arrival. She found the handcrafted sling the wise old woman, Maggie, had given her, and unwrapped the little ribbons. She was surprised to find, inside the sling, a note stitched in twines which read:

ONE IN FOUR ARE BIRDS.

CHAPTER SIX

Fiona spent the months following baby Duriel's birth planning her escape with the children. She knew at least one person from the village believed her about the bird, and that was enough. She taught the older two children to climb the tree, inch by inch, day by day, until she felt sure they could climb down safely. She hid away food and drink and made sure everything was prepared for their journey. Then finally she knew what she must do: wind the bird up so much that he didn't come back for at least three days. That was enough time for her to reach the village with the children before Sicarus would come back, having starved them all and expecting them to be grateful to him for having returned.

That was easy enough. All she had to do was fail to give him his every desire. Be inattentive. When he demanded she got down on her knees to please him she said she was very sorry but couldn't do it at that exact moment because she felt sick after the pregnancy. It worked like clockwork, and in his fury Sicarus turned into the bird, scratching her, pecking her, flapping around, causing a turmoil of unhappiness and abuse. Then he flew off, and this was her chance, her only chance. She told Jegudiel and Gabrielle that they were playing a game to see if their new-found tree-climbing skills could get them to the ground. Jegudiel was eager, but Gabrielle was uncertain. Fiona put baby Duriel in the sling and climbed down after the children; the sling she had also filled with food and treats.

Once on the ground, despite her new injuries she played a game with the children, saying that they would run along the riverbank and catch the moon. The children complained that they were tired, and the moon would always win, but she spurred them on towards hope. By sunrise she let them have a little sleep and some food, and fed baby Duriel, knowing that within twenty-four hours she would be free. On they travelled, and all the way, despite her desire to give up, she encouraged the children to carry on. This time she knew she would succeed as she had her children to look after. Being strong for others makes you far stronger in yourself.

Fiona found the journey even longer this time as the children slowed her down more than she could have imagined. Gabrielle hurt her leg, Jegudiel felt sick and baby Duriel was so heavy in the sling along with all the other supplies that she could hardly carry everything. She struggled on, trying to keep the children entertained and happy. At least this time the bird would not have beat her to it as she felt sure he would have flown away somewhere, happy that he was starving her and the children, happy she would do anything to please him upon his return.

Finally, she reached her village, but to her horror Sicarus was already there, claiming she was an unfit mother and demanding the return of the children. He told the elders of the village, Michael and Peter, that he was entitled to a proper court hearing at the neighbouring village, as was the tradition when villagers argued over where a child should live if their parents separated. Michael and Peter, the village elders, had no option other than to ask the neighbouring village to convene a court hearing for the following week to decide upon the case involving the custody of Gabrielle, Jegudiel and Duriel.

For that week, Fiona felt forever frantic. What if Michael and Peter, the village elders, the rest of the villagers and the neighbouring court believed the bird that she was an unfit mother? What if she had done all this just to lose her children? The thought was unbearable. She went to Sicarus and begged him to take her back, but of course he was unforgiving. "If you want me back," he gloated, "you will have to change your ways."

Fiona nodded and said she would do anything. But whatever she offered, Sicarus wanted more. "Let me get down on my knees for you every day," she suggested, feeling sick to her stomach, but he laughed at her.

"I will expect you to do that morning, noon and night." He grinned. "You will never be allowed to leave the house and the rope ladder will be permanently destroyed. The bark from the tree will be stripped off so it'll be too slippery for you to climb," he continued, enjoying every moment of this new-found power. "You will only be able to speak to the back of my head, and only when I say you can speak to me. You are too unworthy to look at me. The only time I will allow you to look at me is when you are on your knees, and then you must look at me constantly."

Fiona shuddered and agreed. Her life was over now anyway. What did it matter? If the neighbouring village court would give him her children, then her life was not worth living. The only thing that mattered to her now was being with the children, even if it meant having to put up with him.

"You will never come back to this village," he continued to dictate.

Fiona listened as the bird put more and more conditions on her. Each condition was designed to control, humiliate and overpower her, and had no other reason except to provide continuous amusement to the bird. Eventually she could take no more and walked out. She could hear Sicarus calling after her that now she was guaranteed to lose her children and it was all her fault for not going along with his very reasonable request.

She walked straight out of the village and into the forest to Maggie's hut. "Please help," she asked Maggie. "You are the only one who understands about the birds."

Maggie nodded. "You have to learn to believe in yourself," she advised. "And never go back to him or believe what he says under any circumstances."

CHAPTER SEVEN

"A long time ago," Maggie started, "I was married to a bird."

Fiona was amazed and listened intently to Maggie's story.

"When I was a young girl," Maggie continued, "I lived in a neighbouring village similar to this one." Her voice started to shake, and she had a distant, unhappy look in her eye. "My father died suddenly, and my mother didn't cope very well. Together they had traded by running a small school for the children, but after my father died my mother became depressed and wouldn't teach. I had no experience and was only young myself, but I had to take over the school and do two people's jobs because if we didn't continue to trade, we would lose our hut and our place in the village. I resented it and put out the word to other villages that we needed help."

"One day, a charming man from another village turned up. He was experienced in running schools and self-assured, and he really seemed like the answer to our prayers. He said his wife had died and he was left to look after his son, who was close to my age. He spoke fondly to my mother and she appeared to like him at first. I was still young and innocent, and desperately wanted to get my mother back to normal and running the school again, so I could go back to being a young girl with no trade responsibilities. So, I encouraged her to marry him. I made it clear that I was on his side the whole time even though my mother had doubts. I knew she was reluctant to be with him the more she got to know him, but I couldn't understand why. He seemed so charming and kind to her, and it was her only option if we were to remain in our village and live the life we had always lived. My mother wanted us to leave the village and find a new life, just the two of us, but I wouldn't hear of it. So she went ahead and married him to please me. We were a happy family for a while, my mother, the teacher and I. His son didn't live with us and had remained with his grandmother in the neighbouring village."

"But slowly that changed," Maggie continued. "I used to see strange shadows in our hut at night and hear screeching noises. Then I started to notice my mother was scratched and had cuts and bruises over her arms and legs, and she started to look depressed again. When I talked to her about it she clammed up, so I talked to her husband, the teacher. He was called Trollos. He told me that my mother was self-harming, but I found it difficult to believe. My instincts told me Trollos was hurting her, but everyone tried to convince me he was a good man and was helping my mother but I didn't, by then, trust him. So, I decided to try and find out his background and a bit more about him, and I went to visit his son in the neighbouring village."

Maggie cleared her throat. "The son confirmed my fears. His father appeared charming but deep down was an evil man. Trollos had attacked his own son and left his village to be a teacher in another village. Trollos had abandoned his own child, who had only lost his mother to a horrible accident a year before. He was the most beautiful boy I had ever laid eyes on. At nineteen he was three years older than me, and tall with broad shoulders and black eyes."

Fiona gulped. She knew what was coming next.

"I fell in love with him straight away, and he wanted to marry me and agreed come back to live with me in my mother's hut where we could all be together. My mother was sad when she found out about our relationship, but I didn't understand why. I thought maybe she just couldn't be happy and didn't want me to find happiness either. We argued constantly, and I told her that she clearly didn't love me, and I loved her husband's son and wanted to marry him. Trollos' son was called Stigmus and he had a most amazing talent."

"One-night Stigmus had shown me a secret, how he could magically fly around the night sky, and I thought I was the luckiest girl in the world. I tried to explain to my mother that he had magical powers and would look after me forever, but she remained unhappy about the forthcoming marriage and then announced that she wouldn't be able to allow us to live in the family hut, and neither would Trollos. If I insisted on marrying him, I would no longer be her daughter. I was shocked by her harsh words."

"I remember seeing her face, agonised and distorted, and noticing even more scratches up her arms. Her husband Trollos had hold of her hand a little too tight as she was speaking to me and was smiling. He hadn't even congratulated us on our engagement. I could tell my mother was torn and was doing what her husband, not she, wanted, but I didn't understand why she hadn't stood up to him. I do now, but I didn't then, and that was the last time I saw my mother, so I never got the chance to tell her I loved her or understood."

Maggie looked to the ground. She shuddered. "I told my mother she was selfish and heartless, and I would still marry Stigmus and go and live with my lovely future husband as far away from her and her creepy husband as I could. I remember thinking at the time how odd it was that my own lovely future husband's father was a monster, and how different they were. I didn't understand how someone so lovely could have come from that."

"But later I realised how wrong I was. After we wed my new husband was kind to me, or so I thought, and found us a hut many miles away from my mother, miles away from anyone. When I heard my mother had died by her own hand, I didn't believe it and wanted to go back to the village, but Stigmus told me I shouldn't look back and refused to fly me back. It was at least a week's walk to my village, and at that time I didn't feel up to such a long walk. I thought my husband was trying to protect me."

Maggie sighed. "It didn't occur to me until later how isolated I had become. I saw no one except my husband, but more and more he started to fly off for longer periods of time. At first just a few hours, then a whole day, then several days."

CHAPTER EIGHT

Fiona listened to Maggie's story with sadness. Maggie told her how her own husband turned into a bird in the beginning, and it was thrilling as they flew beneath the twinkling stars and the midnight sky. Maggie was happy and didn't think too deeply about how her mother had suffered and died because of the man Maggie herself had introduced her to. Her mother's scratched arms and the shadows and screeching noises made no sense until Maggie started to experience them herself. Her story was spookily familiar. An accidental scratch, an angry scratch, a deliberate scratch, a torturous scratch, a sadistic scratch coupled with multiple kicks and sharp pecks in intimate places which had otherwise only known gentleness. It was during one such attack that Maggie suffered such dreadful internal injuries that she lost her unborn baby and was unable ever to conceive again.

Fiona could feel the sadness in Maggie's story. Maggie went on to tell her that Stigmus would later begin to torment her about being barren and told her she was not woman enough for him. He started to leave her for longer and longer periods of time, sometimes without food. He told her that if he didn't come back for a week, she should assume he was dead and ask for mercy and charity from the nearby village. Maggie knew, like all villagers, that each village had to be self-sufficient and each villager had to work and have a trade for the village to function and flourish. Whilst the villagers could look after their own elderly and sick, they could never support outsiders unless it was a matter of life and death. For this reason, all villages had a rule that if an outsider asked them for charity and mercy, they would be taken care of. However, if the outsider was not genuinely in need and it wasn't a matter of life and death, or there was another person or village who could reasonably be expected to look after them, then there would be serious consequences. Generally, this involved locking the outsider up in a hut and treating them like an animal.

Maggie's husband didn't come back for seven days and beyond. Maggie knew she would surely starve. She lasted ten days until she crawled to the nearest village and begged them for mercy, which they freely gave. She told them her husband had died and there was no other person who could be expected to look after her. Maggie started to settle in the village and helped to look after the animals. She started to feel part of the village and was given more responsibility. After six months she was out one day looking for a lost animal when she received a hard blow to her head. Stigmus had hit her with a large rock and dragged her back to their old hut miles away from the village.

When Maggie awoke, she heard the sound of a crying baby. Her husband had brought her back to his hut where he now lived with his second wife and their new baby. His second wife, Maria, had become ill from all the beatings she had been given and he needed someone to look after her and the baby. Maggie was told that unless she looked after and accepted them, he would send her back to the village and she would be locked up by them because she had taken their mercy and charity when it wasn't a genuine matter of life and death and her husband had been there to support her all along. She had committed fraud on them.

Maggie froze. She knew her choice was imprisonment at the village, to be treated like an animal, or living in a cruel and adulterous relationship. She wanted to choose imprisonment to get as far away from her husband as she could, until she saw the state of his second wife. Maria was at death's door and the baby was starving, neglected; his tiny lips were blue. Maggie's heart went out to them. She discovered to her horror that the second wife, Maria lost a lot of blood following the birth and was constantly tired. She had started to scold her husband because he wasn't helping with the baby. At first, he pushed her away, then hit her, then punched her, but it would not shut her up. Stigmus had then reached for his hunting knife to threaten her, as he used to do with Maggie. But unlike the many times when threatening someone with a knife had worked, on this occasion it didn't. Maria continued to berate him. He couldn't allow that, so there was only one thing he could do to shut her up for good. He cut her tongue out. She never nagged him again.

But the injury made her even more ill and unable to look after the baby. So, Maggie was brought back and told to take care of them both, which she did. Stigmus took it in turns sleeping with his two wives. Maggie planned to leave him and take Maria with her when she and the baby were nursed back to health, but then Maria felt unable to leave. Maggie understood why. Sometimes it is too difficult to leave and just easier to stay. Even though staying is unbearable, the alternative is too frightening to even comprehend when you have lost everything.

CHAPTER NINE

Fiona was filled with pity. She had known Maggie all her life and never imagined that she had lived such a sorrowful life. Maggie disclosed that when she did finally leave her husband, his second wife and child remained. Maggie went back to the village that had previously given her mercy and charity and had to accept that they would imprison her for fraud. They locked her up for over a year, and during that time Maggie became an elective mute, out of respect for Maria who was unable to get away. After a few years of wandering she resolved to find a village that didn't know of her background and try and teach the children to beware of the birds and began to speak again. But of course, the village decided her teachings were too unorthodox and she had to leave and build her own hut in the forest.

Fiona started to worry. *One in four are birds* was Maggie's message to her. How could her own village have cast Maggie out simply for speaking the truth? How many birds were in Fiona's village and she hadn't realised it? How many people were suffering in silence and too frightened to leave? For a few moments Fiona had forgotten about her own horrible situation with the court case and Sicarus trying to have her children taken away from her, as she was feeling the pain of the many which included Maggie, her mother, and Maria who had all suffered at the hands of the birds. Then her own reality set in once again. Before hearing Maggie's story, she had been begging Sicarus to have her back, to avoid the court case and the risk of losing Gabrielle, Jegudiel and Duriel. She shuddered. She knew she could never go back and had to face this future even though it was as scary as living with a bird. If she could find the strength to finally stand up to him and win, she would be able to help others. But the thought of standing up to him in front of the court made her cry.

There were eight more days until the court case, but it felt like eight months or even eight years. Fiona tried hard to settle back into the village with the children, and even tried to resume her occupation of looking after the village animals but found it impossible to concentrate on anything other than the court case. It constantly occupied her mind and prevented her from sleeping or functioning in any way. Hour by hour she sat and cried, visualising how it would feel if Sicarus were allowed to take her children away and she never got to see them. Each time she saw their angelic faces her heart wanted to stop beating so she would never have to face the day of judgement.

Seven days before the court case, she thought about running away from the village. But where could they run to? How could she survive with three young children? How would the children cope? They had been through so much already. It was pointless. The children were just beginning to settle into the village and form friendships with the other children and a relationship with her parents, whose hut they were all staying in until after the hearing.

Six days before the court case, she could not face the prospect of her children being taken away from her and forced to live with Sicarus, who would be cruel to them. He would no doubt punish them to hurt her, and the thought of that made her cry. She thought perhaps they would all be better off dead, and she wondered how she could arrange this within the next six days. Her mind raced and envisaged all sorts of horrors, but of course she couldn't entertain the idea of killing her own children for long, and after crying some more decided she had no option other than to face Sicarus and win.

Five days before the court case, Sicarus turned up in the village to gather his evidence. He insisted the village elders, Peter and Michael, examine the children to prove his allegations that Fiona was an unfit mother and present their findings to the court on his behalf. Fiona watched in horror as Sicarus demanded Michael and Peter note all the injuries the children had. Gabrielle had a cut foot from walking on a rock during their escape. Jegudiel had grazed his knees from climbing down the tree and Duriel was slightly thinner for not eating enough on the arduous journey back to the village. "See how she has harmed them!" shouted Sicarus, smiling selfishly. "The court will certainly rule in my favour!"

Four days before the court case, Fiona didn't want to get out of bed. She hadn't slept again, and she was scared. Her parents talked her round and told her she must get up and look after the children or surely Sicarus would be back, gathering more evidence. "He is still controlling me now even though he is not here," sobbed Fiona. She got up and looked after the children, hoping that the days would pass, and the court case would soon be here. By dusk she regretted that and hoped it would never come and the days would stand still. But the days and nights passed in their own time and at their own pace, despite any hopes and fears Fiona had.

Three days before the court case, Sicarus turned up again, this time to offer Fiona a settlement. The children would live with him in his house made of sticks in the forest, and Fiona could either live with them as his servant and abandon all rights to be their mother, or she could remain in the village, be declared an unfit mother and see them once a year when it was convenient for him. Fiona could not speak, but he told her that when the court declared her an unfit mother, he would be employing another servant to look after the children, so she would lose this very reasonable offer if she didn't act now and take it gratefully. He also reminded her that once declared unfit mother by the court, she would never get the opportunity to see the children again. Luckily, Fiona fainted and was unable to accept his offer.

Two days before the court case, Fiona decided that if she was going to lose the children, she should make their last memories with their mother special for them, and she resolved not to cry in front of them or get depressed, and to give them the best last couple of days she could. She took them out to the forest with a picnic, and they ate it together and played with the wild animals. The children ran around the forest without a care in the world and Fiona smiled at them behind her tears.

CHAPTER TEN

On the day before the court case, Fiona received an unexpected offer from one of the village boys who had no wife. He offered to marry her and then they would be given their own hut, which would look good for the court case. Fiona was delighted, so she agreed to let the boy take her and the children out for the day. He took them to the forest and bought them food and treats. Fiona thought they were having a perfect day and thanked him with a smile.

"My pleasure," he replied. "And now I have made you smile, there is something you can do for me." And he tried to push her to her knees.

Fiona's heart sank as she noticed his beady black eyes. She dared not upset him. If he attacked her, she would surely be covered in cuts and bruises at the court hearing tomorrow. No one would believe she had met another bird, and Sicarus would probably tell the court that she had been self-harming, which would mean that she would surely be declared an unfit mother.

How could she have been so stupid as to have allowed herself to get in this situation? What was wrong with her? Was there something written on her face to show the birds that she was easy prey? She took a deep breath and decided she had no option other than to give this bird what he required and then get the hell out of there. She swallowed hard, checked the children were still asleep on the forest floor, exhausted after a fun day, and dropped to her knees.

Afterwards she politely thanked the boy, who was called Thomas, for taking them all out for a fun day in the forest, woke the children and went back to her parents' hut to prepare for court the following day.

Her parents would not be attending with her as they had agreed to look after the children. After Fiona had put the children to bed, she kissed them and watched their sleeping, angelic faces. She panicked that she would never see them again and sat watching them all night. There was no point even trying to sleep as she was so scared it had overtaken everything else in her brain.

Finally, the morning of the court case arrived. The sun was shining, and Fiona could not understand how the sun could shine or the rest of the world could carry on with its everyday business, as everything stood still for her. In the past she had heard about village wars and how the men went off to fight and never came back to their families, and she knew how they must have felt. Goodbye to everything safe and loved as you leave to fight and possibly die, with no freedom to choose your own fate: someone has forced you into a terrible situation and all you can do is go along with it, do what you can to survive and hope it is over soon.

Fiona travelled to the neighbouring village where the court was to be held with the village elders, Peter, Michael and several others from her village including the boy Thomas she had gone out with to the forest the day before. She remained polite but distant with him. "Please let me just get through today first," she whispered to him as she pulled her hand away from his when he tried to grab her.

"All right then," Thomas replied, "but I will want you to make it up to me."

When they arrived at the neighbouring village, Sicarus was already there. The sight of him dressed up in his finery, looking smug, made Fiona let out an involuntary cry. Sicarus scowled when he saw Thomas, the village boy with Fiona. "I feel sorry for you, putting up with her." He pointed at Fiona with such contempt he couldn't even say her name.

Thomas' response wasn't much better. "Well, mate, someone's got to take her on for the good of the village."

They shared a smile, then Sicarus sniggered. "Throw her back my way when you have had enough."

Fiona wanted to run away, but she bowed her head in shame and said nothing.

She looked over to where the court had convened. It was a large temporary hut with no colour and no door, standing boldly at the centre of the village with solemnity and importance. These temporary huts were often used for village celebrations, weddings and the birth of a baby, even funerals, and decorated with brightly coloured flowers and leaves. But today it was bare. Today it would decide the fate of Gabrielle, Jegudiel and Duriel, and of course Fiona. She did not recognise any of the three villagers who had been given the power and authority to give judgement. Two men and a woman. The woman seemed to have a kind face, but the men looked fairly severe and Fiona wondered if they could be birds. If they were she didn't stand a chance. Perhaps she should just give in now and walk into the forest, never to be seen again. She could be food for the wild animals; at least her life might serve some purpose after all. But instead she entered the temporary hut and stood before them.

She had to stand there asking the court to allow her to keep the children she had given birth to, that she had grown within her body and protected when the bird attacked her. She had already decided to tell the court it was Sicarus who attacked her and not mention his transformation into a bird. She didn't know whether anyone in the courtroom was a bird or would believe her if they didn't know about the birds. Sicarus denied attacking her and told the court that she had in fact attacked him. He went on to say that she then harmed herself and the children. Fiona frantically hoped no one would believe him, but Sicarus was able to prove the children had some injuries after Fiona had left him. She tried to explain that the injuries occurred during their escape through the forest, but she was unsure whether anyone believed her.

The day dragged by. Sicarus seemed so believable that she thought she was bound to lose her children. This in itself made her feel more nervous, and so uptight and stressed that she thought she was surely coming across as neurotic and therefore an unfit mother. She felt she was playing right into his hands and there was nothing she could do to stop herself. She looked at the three people tasked to judge her children's future. They had never even met Gabrielle, Jegudiel and Duriel, so how could it possibly be fair that they could decide their fate?

After the three strangers had heard all the evidence, they went off to chat among themselves and make their decision. They took what seemed like many hours but was probably less than an hour. During that time Fiona paced up and down, biting the skin off her lip with her teeth. She remembered the bird pacing one of the first times he became angry, and she drew blood, wondering if taking skin off your lip could be classed as harming yourself. Everything was so blurred in her head she almost wondered if she would soon turn into a bird herself and was indeed capable of all the horrible things Sicarus had accused her of in court.

Her head was still whirling when the three announced their verdict. There were lots of words floating around the temporary hut, but Fiona only heard a few: "…children to stay in the village with her."

CHAPTER ELEVEN

She wasn't sure if she had heard correctly until Sicarus stood up, shouted at the three decision makers that he would be back, and stormed out of the temporary hut in a fit of temper. Peter and Michael, the village elders, turned to her and told her they always knew she would win, and Thomas the boy from her village beamed and tried to put his arm around her, but she backed away. "I feel so tired," she said to Peter and Michael. "Can you take me back to the village please, just us?" They nodded and rose to their feet, leaving Thomas and the other villagers behind, telling them to give Fiona some space. Thomas was clearly furious but didn't want to appear unreasonable in front of the others.

When Fiona got back to her parents' hut she was overjoyed and kissed the children. She thanked her parents for looking after them and expected to have the best sleep of her life. But she still couldn't sleep as the trauma of the court case and all the lies Sicarus had told about her still haunted her. When eventually she slept, she had fragmented nightmares where two birds were pecking at her eyes, one on each side, and had made her blind. She opened her eyes and saw nothing but blackness, and felt her cheeks wet with tears.

Over the next few weeks Fiona did her best to avoid Thomas, the boy from the village, and mostly stayed in her parents' hut. She started to help her mother look after the village animals again and gradually took over her old occupation, freeing her mother up to assist her father as she had previously done by making animal pens and fences for the village. Her mother was not able to collect, chop or shape the wood, or indeed dig holes in the earth for the wood to stand secure, but she was able to weave vines around it to make the fences more stable. Her father was a man of few words but was loyal and kind to her mother. He was very traditional and mainly spoke to Fiona through her mother. "Your father thinks you should look for the escaped animals in the forest today," her mother would declare on behalf of her husband, and Fiona would inevitably go along with his advice.

But a few weeks after the court case, her mother stated, "Your father wants you to finish the fence he is building as he needs a rest today."

Fiona looked puzzled. Her father never rested. But she obediently finished the fence even though it was hard manual labour and took her all day without stopping for a break. When she was finished, she ran home to her mother to tell her to let her father know it was completed. She was so proud of herself for finally being able to be a help rather than a hindrance. Most adult daughters did not have to still live in their parents' hut, and she knew she was an embarrassment to them within the village. But when she arrived at their hut with a spring in her step, she knew something dreadful had happened.

She wandered into the hut and heard her mother weeping. Then she saw her father. He was lying still in the bed with his eyes closed. His face was grey and lifeless. He looked different; not like her father but someone else, someone not full of life. He was just an empty shell; his spirit had fled his body. Fiona fell to her knees. Her life had changed yet again; nothing ever seemed to stay still for her and let her have more than a few days' happiness. Trauma after trauma was all her life seemed to consist of. Her father's death would have a profound effect upon her mother and their village life. The hut they were living in was a substantial hut in the heart of the village because her father had an important occupation building and maintaining the village fences. Her mother might not be able to keep the hut if she had to ask the village for charity and was unable to earn her keep. Fiona didn't think she would be able to do everything her father did as the role would need a strong, muscular body, and even though she had managed today she doubted her physical strength would hold up for long. She felt sad that all she could think about was her and her mother's future when she should instead have been concentrating on grieving.

Fiona's mother fell apart following the funeral in the village's temporary hut, a hut very similar to the one in the neighbouring village where her court case had been heard. She shuddered at the thought of what she had been through. Her mother was unable to work. She couldn't even assist with Fiona's occupation of looking after the village animals, so Fiona had to do this as well as attempting to build and maintain all the village fences as her father used to. Fiona was exhausted, working all the daylight hours and leaving the children with her mother and other women in the village when they were not being taught by the village teachers. Despite all the effort she put in some of the fences started to look as weary as Fiona, and eventually they fell down.

The village elders, Peter and Michael approached Fiona a few months later about her work. "We know you are trying your best," Michael said gravely. "But the fact is we are getting complaints about the state of the fences and the number of animals escaping."

"We have decided," continued Peter, "that we need to find a new fence builder from another village to take over your father's occupation. It will free you up to look after the animals. You can stay in your hut until we find a replacement for your father, but then we will need to offer him your father's hut. We can house you and your mother in one of the charity huts on the edge of the village. We are very sorry, but village business must come first."

Fiona turned pale. All her hard work over the last few months had been in vain. All the times she'd had to leave the children in the care of others had come to nothing. But the worst shock was still to come when, a few weeks later, she discovered who had been given her father's occupation and hut. Sicarus.

Fiona's blood ran cold. Sicarus had cleverly found a way never to let her go, where he could watch her every move and constantly be around her and in her and the children's lives. After the court case was over he had disappeared into the forest and Fiona naively thought she would never see him again. She had only had a short time on her own without him and now she was trapped again. Worse still, he was stalking her with the consent and blessing of her village, the people who had helped bring her up and the place where she had previously felt safe. But not now. She wanted to run away, to hide in the forest and scream. Her mind raced as to what she could do to prevent this. The court in the neighbouring village had declared it was in the children's best interests to live in the village with her. She hadn't for one second contemplated that Sicarus would be able to live there too. If she had anticipated that, then she would have asked the court to rule that the children lived with her and he was not allowed to live in the same village. She had heard of these types of rulings before but had also heard that they were only made in rare cases. Even if she had asked for such a ruling, she felt sure they wouldn't have granted it. She was simply stuck. Stuck forever in the worst way.

Fiona's world was closing in on her, swirling and tormenting, laughing at her. How bitterly she regretted the day she fell in love with Sicarus' attentions.

Sicarus moved into her parents' hut the following week. She was given one day to move herself, her mother, the children and all their belongings out before he took up residence. It took her all day to move everything. The boy from the village, Thomas, offered to help, but she refused. No doubt he had his own agenda and would want something from her in return. *Trust no one*, she thought to herself. *Accept no favours and you will not have to be put in a position where someone wants something from you that you do not wish to give. Be independent.*

She cleared out her parents' hut and found some crumbs and dirt left on the floor. Her memory went back to when she had scoured the floor of the house made of sticks when Sicarus had abandoned them without food, and she had given the children mouldy and unclean crumbs. She wished she could erase such memories from her brain as they always stopped her dead in her tracks. She felt like smearing the hut walls with the dirt, but she didn't. She refused to sink to his level and try to seek revenge or punish him. So she cleaned out the hut and left it fresh and tidy. For anyone else she would have picked flowers to welcome the new occupant, but she was unable to go that far. Sicarus was not welcome.

CHAPTER TWELVE

Weary, Fiona went to the charity hut on the edge of the village which was now her home. Her mother was sitting still in a chair while the children played around her, trying to attract her attention, but she was oblivious to them. At the tender age of six, Gabrielle was attempting to look after her two younger brothers. Jegudiel was now four and Duriel was still only a baby, but they needed an adult to meet their needs. Fiona felt guilty. She resolved to try and sort out proper arrangements for them and noted that her mother was no longer able to assist. Bereavement can kill or cure a person and she worried about her mother, particularly now as she had just lost her home. Fiona blamed Sicarus for this. He was destroying her mother to destroy her.

The following day, she bumped into him in the village. She was taking the children to be looked after by another mother so she didn't have to trouble her own mother while she was working. With having to organise moving huts the previous day, she had neglected her occupation of looking after the village animals and they were looking sad and underfed, with unkempt bedding. Fiona's shoulders were heavy as she was carrying Duriel in one arm and holding Jegudiel's chubby little hand on the other side. Sicarus seemed to spring out of nowhere and almost knocked her off her feet. She felt sick that he had touched her.

"You want to watch where you are going," he laughed at her. Then he forcibly removed Duriel from her arms. "My son!" he proclaimed. "Daddy has missed you!" Then he started throwing Duriel up in the air, the way he used to with Jegudiel when he played with him, normally after he had hurt Fiona so badly that she was unable to care for him and Gabrielle. This made baby Duriel chuckle, a deep, spontaneous, contagious chuckle that immediately spread to Jegudiel and Gabrielle. Only Fiona remained still, unable to catch the laughter.

The older two children wanted turns at being thrown into the air and jumped up and down impatiently, shouting, "Daddy, Daddy, my turn!"

Sicarus looked at them and struck another cruel blow. "Your mummy won't let you, my poor children. She wants to stop your fun. Horrible Mummy."

Fiona sunk as the children pleaded with her not to stop their fun and to let them have a turn with Daddy. How could she say no? So she stood there awkwardly while the man who had harmed her in every way possible pretended to care about his children by making them laugh.

"Daddy has to go now to do your grandad's work," Sicarus told the children. "The work is easy and will only take me an hour a day at the most, so I will have lots of time to see you and play with you." He smiled boastfully.

"Daddy, we have moved – do you know where we live now?" Gabrielle asked him innocently.

"Of course, I do." Sicarus beamed. "Daddy knows everything about Mummy. I will come and see you all later."

The hairs on the back of Fiona's neck were still sticking up as she approached the other mother's hut and asked her to please look after the children for the rest of the day, so Fiona could concentrate on her work.

After a long day of cleaning, feeding and looking after the animals, Fiona returned to the other mother's hut to collect the children. "Their father collected them ten minutes ago," the woman, called Beverly, explained. "They had been under my feet all day, along with my own children. I didn't know when you were coming for them, and their father not only offered to take them but my own children as well, so I could catch up with all the things I needed to do. What a kind man!"

Fiona couldn't listen any more, so she muttered her thanks and scurried off in search of her children.

She ran to her parents' old hut, but no one was there. She noticed that Sicarus had painted the door a different colour, bright red, and had dug up the pretty flowers her father had planted at the front. The hut looked more aggressive now and masculine, no longer the sweet home of her childhood. Fiona searched the village for signs of her children but found no clues. She was beside herself. Dusk was creeping in and she worried constantly that Sicarus had taken the children for good and she would never see her baby angels again. She began to cry.

Finally, after what seemed an eternity, the children were returned, and came tumbling through the door excited, tired and very hungry. "Daddy said you would have food waiting for us," Jegudiel cried when he saw the empty table. Fiona hid her tears and hurriedly prepared some food for the impatient children. Her instincts told her that Sicarus was still lurking about outside somewhere in the shadows, watching her every move.

Sicarus turned up at Fiona's charity hut on the outskirts of the village at different times for the next few weeks. There was no pattern as to when to expect him, and indeed whenever someone walked past the hut she jumped and thought it would be Sicarus. All Fiona knew was that the children seemed pleased to see him. She really didn't want to talk to him, but felt she needed to in order to establish a regular pattern for the children. She generally had to take care of the animals first thing in the morning and again in the early afternoon for a few hours each time, and had to rely on the other mother, Beverly, who now seemed more and more reluctant, when the children were not at school. It meant that Fiona was at home with the children around midday for a couple of hours, and each evening. So she finally plucked up the courage and tried to speak to Sicarus about the children.

She knew he was only spending about an hour a day on his occupation, and stupidly thought he could see the children when she was busy with hers. How wrong she was. When she suggested this, he just laughed at her and snorted, "I will never be a babysitter for your children. You will have to sort out sitters yourself to allow you to carry out your work. I know how ill your mother is, how she sits still in the chair every day, unable to look after your children. I know she has lost everything including her hut, which has been given to me. I hope she suffers and dies, and you will be left alone with nothing and no one. I will turn up to see the children only when I want to, and only to prevent you spending time with them when you want to. I will destroy you and everyone around you, including your children. That is a promise." He whispered the last words to her and then barged into her hut and pretended to be sad, telling the children that he had come to take them on a magical trip to the beach but couldn't because Mummy was horrible and wouldn't let them go. The children were naturally upset, and Jegudiel even started to hit at her legs, shouting that she was horrible.

Fiona saw Sicarus many times during the next few weeks, in various places around the village. He was there when she took the children to and from school and the other mother Beverley's hut. He was there when she was taking care of the village animals. He was there outside her charity hut when she returned home. But he never once took the children. He just called to them, telling them their mother was horrible and wouldn't let them have fun with their daddy, and then watched them become upset and take out their emotions on Fiona. On one occasion she tried to call his bluff and stupidly spoke directly to the children, telling them they were free to go with him and she wasn't stopping them, and she wanted them to have a nice time with their daddy. But Sicarus spoke loudly over her, telling the children not to listen to Mummy's lies and it was her and only her preventing them having fun.

The children were left feeling betrayed, unwanted and confused, and Fiona felt she could say no more as it would make it worse.

CHAPTER THIRTEEN

There was another death in the village. This time a young man with a young family had died in the forest. He had apparently been attacked by an animal. Rumours started that it might not have been one of the wild animals from deep in the forest but one of the village animals that hadn't been looked after properly by Fiona and had gone insane. The young man's widow was devastated, and the temporary hut in the middle of the village was used to hold his funeral feast. Fiona wasn't invited. Sicarus was chief mourner and stood by the widow's side throughout the funeral and played with her children. The widow, called Phyllis, cried on his broad shoulders.

A few weeks later the widow came to Fiona's charity hut on the outskirts of the village. Fiona's mother remained sitting still in her chair as Fiona invited Phyllis into her hut. "I've come on behalf of Sicarus," the widow began. "We have grown closer recently and I want you to know that as a mother I am completely disgusted by your actions.

How can you stop your children from seeing their father?" Then she sobbed, "My children would give anything to have their father back in their lives, but they never will."

Fiona tried to explain that Sicarus was the one refusing to see his children, that it was all just a sick game to him and he was a bird who had hurt her, but the widow retorted that Sicarus had told her Fiona would say this, that Fiona was an unfit mother and she would help Sicarus to ensure that the children would be taken away from her. "As for a bird that hurts you," spat the widow, holding back her anger, "that is utter nonsense. Birds are beautiful and magical and would never hurt anyone. Sicarus is kind and strong and I know he would never have hurt you. I know him well enough by now to know that you are the liar and shouldn't be allowed to have your children. I am going to help Sicarus go back to the court, and this time he will win. The court won't believe any more of your lies." With that she stormed out of the hut, and once again Fiona's instincts told her that Sicarus was lurking outside in the shadows, listening to every word. She cried well into the night.

Sicarus helped by the widow Phyllis applied once again to the court in the neighbouring village for custody of Gabrielle, Jegudiel and Duriel, claiming that Fiona was an unfit mother. When Fiona heard this, she wept bitterly. The court hearing was again set for eight days' time. And so began the worst eight days of Fiona's life. Again.

Even though she knew what to expect – the unadorned temporary hut in the rising boldly in the middle of the neighbouring village, the three strangers waiting there to decide the whole lifetime and upbringing of her children whom they had never met, the agony of waiting for the court's determination – the court case the second time around was just as scary. Perhaps scarier, because now Sicarus had the widow as his supporter and Fiona had no one. Two against one. He would surely win this time; if not because the number of witnesses was weighted against her, but simply by the law of averages.

🪶

Seven days before the court case, she again considered running away with the children. They were a little older now and had learned a great deal about survival over the past few months. Gabrielle had become used to looking after her younger brothers, and Jegudiel and Duriel had in turn become used to looking after themselves. They had all grown up very quickly, even being left for short periods of time with Fiona's mother, who sat still in her chair. But if Fiona ran it would be no life for the children, and anyway Sicarus would surely find them. He had promised to destroy her and everything around her, and she believed now that he would be successful.

Six days before the court case, Fiona wanted to die. She didn't feel able to go through the whole process again of being accused of being an unfit mother, and the risk of losing her children. She had only just felt secure that they would remain with her after the last court hearing, and the thought of losing them now was just as incomprehensible as it had been then; to have something given with one hand and then taken away by the other. But she couldn't kill herself now; she had to stand up and be accused and hope somehow that she would get to keep her beautiful angels forever. But if she lost them, her life would be not worth living.

Five days before the court case, the widow Phyllis turned up to gather evidence for Sicarus. She took one look at Fiona's mother sitting in her chair and told Fiona she and Sicarus would ensure that the court was aware that Fiona was using unsuitable babysitters. Fiona looked at her mother sitting on her wooden chair with her head in her hands. An old woman in sorrow on the threshold of eternity. Her heart ached. She wished she could help her mother, but she couldn't. All her energy had been drained by Sicarus and the court case. "Tell the court what you want," Fiona whispered, unable to take her eyes off her mother. That night her mother joined her husband and passed away in her sleep.

Four days before the court case, Fiona didn't want to get out of bed. Her mother had gone. Her father had gone. Her children might soon be gone. But she had to get up. She had to plan a funeral and lay her mother's body to rest. She had to get the children up and look after them before school started. If they missed school Sicarus might accuse her of being an unfit mother. Then she had to carry out her occupation of looking after the village animals. If she failed to do this, Sicarus might accuse her of being an unfit mother and neglecting the animals. Every waking moment of her day she was thinking about Sicarus and how he was still hurting and controlling her.

Three days before the court case, the widow Phyllis turned up offering a settlement. If Fiona would accept that she was an unfit mother, they would allow her to see her children again when it suited them. Phyllis was hoping

Sicarus would propose, and if he did, she did not wish to be saddled with Fiona's children and had her heart set on a child-free honeymoon by the ocean. The widow Phyllis' own mother was getting old, and whilst she would look after her grandchildren, Phyllis did not wish to burden her with Fiona's children, particularly as they wouldn't be very well behaved, having had such an appalling upbringing with Fiona as their mother. Oh yes, Sicarus had told her everything; they had no secrets. She knew all about Fiona harming her children and herself and trying to blame it all on poor Sicarus. Fiona politely declined the offer and asked the widow to leave. She missed her mother.

Two days before the court case, Fiona decided the children needed some fun. They had just lost their grandmother and might soon lose their mother. She would give them a lovely last couple of days to remember, and this time it would not involve going to the forest with any horrible boys from the village. It would just be Fiona and the children. A family unit; a happy family with no birds to control and hurt them. The day she spent in the forest with her children was one of the best days of Fiona's life. They ran and jumped, played games and laughed so much together that it gave Gabrielle hiccups, Jegudiel became dizzy with dancing and baby Duriel, who had only just learned to stand up, took his first steps. Everyone cheered. They had a delicious picnic, and everyone fell asleep with the sun shining on their faces.

CHAPTER FOURTEEN

The day before the court case, Fiona had another unexpected offer. One of her parents' friends, Timulus, turned up at her hut to tell her how sorry he was about her mother's death. His wife had died a couple of years ago and he knew how she felt. He then told Fiona that he knew of her court case and might be able to help her, because he sometimes sat as a judge in the temporary hut in their village and he knew how these cases went. It would help her case if she were married, and although he was nearly thirty years older than her he would agree to marry her as a favour to her parents. "Of course," he continued, his beady black eyes shining, "I would need a favour or two from you in return." And he tried to push her to her knees.

Fiona stood up and stood firm. "No thank you," she replied politely. "I don't need a man or a husband." And then she said under her breath, "And I am never going to associate with a bird again. Goodbye."

The day of the second court case arrived. Fiona again travelled with the village elders, Peter, Michael and some of the other villagers. Thomas, the boy from the village didn't come this time, and neither did Timulus, her parents' friend. Fiona again saw the unadorned temporary hut rising proudly in the centre of the neighbouring village, with Sicarus standing outside in his smart clothes, smirking. She couldn't see the widow Phyllis and assumed she had already gone inside. Fiona felt sick. Judgement Day had come again. She walked into the temporary hut behind Sicarus, her eyes fixed on the back of his head. She knew every hair well as he had insisted for many years that she only spoke to him from behind, proclaiming that she was too undeserving to look at his face. How she hated that sight, and indeed the rest of his body. A body that she had once found attractive, but now repulsed her. How he had made her fear his every move and made her get down on her knees every evening just to try and appease his vile temper.

As she walked in, Fiona saw the three strangers there to decide the upbringing of Gabrielle, Jegudiel and Duriel. They were a different set of strangers this time. Somehow, she had expected the same ones, and it made her panic. The previous ones had believed her. These three were sure to believe Sicarus and the widow. They knew nothing about her. They knew nothing about her children. Fiona could hardly breathe.

Sicarus once again began with numerous lies about Fiona and her fitness to parent. She had harmed the children and herself. She had heard that before, many times. Then he alleged she had killed her parents because she was mad and had killed her animals, tortured them and caused them to go insane, which resulted in the widow Phyllis' husband being killed. Fiona looked around the court in shame, desperately hoping no one would believe him. If they did, not only would she lose her children, but she would be unable to return to her village. She looked for Phyllis who had helped Sicarus come up with these lies, but she wasn't there.

Then it was Fiona's turn to speak to the strangers. This time she not only told them about how Sicarus had harmed her and the children, but also, as unbelievable as it sounded, about him turning into a bird. She wanted to tell the truth, but she knew how insane it would sound to someone who had no experience of birds. After she had finished speaking, she saw their puzzled faces. Her heart sunk. She shouldn't have told them after all. They wouldn't believe her and would think she was the one who had gone insane and harmed herself and everyone around her. She sat down with her head in her hands, sitting very still, the way her mother had done before her death. She would be sure to join her mother and father later, perhaps tonight after the children had been taken away from her.

She didn't hear another person quietly enter the room until that person had started to timidly speak to the court. Fiona looked round and saw the widow, Phyllis, her face scratched with three bright red tracks of blood. Talon marks. Her arms were bruised purple and black, having been savagely pecked.

"It's true," Phyllis began. "Sicarus is a bird who is capable of the most horrific violence. He has made me suffer badly. I am so sorry, Fiona, that I didn't believe you and sided with him. Please forgive me."

Fiona nodded with tears in her eyes.

"Sicarus cares nothing for his children," the widow Phyllis, continued. "He only wanted them to hurt you. He is completely obsessed with you and is fixated on destroying you."

Sicarus started shouting at the widow and the three strangers, even before they had given their judgement. He began pacing angrily, and by the time the three strangers were able to give their verdict that once again the children should remain in the village with Fiona, Sicarus had spikes protruding from the skin of his back.

The court then added another provision of its own motion. Sicarus would never be allowed to apply to the court again in respect of any orders regarding Gabrielle, Jegudiel or Duriel, and he would not be allowed to live in the village where Fiona and the children lived.

Fiona's heart leapt. Finally, she was free.

Sicarus moved out of her parents' hut and Fiona moved back in. She continued with her occupation of looking after the village animals, and Maggie and Fiona between them took over her father's occupation of making fences and animal pens. Later, as they grew older, the children helped out after school.

Although Sicarus was forced to leave the village, he didn't go far. He built a house of sticks in the forest about a mile away from where Fiona and the children lived. Fiona's instincts told her he was still coming into the village at night, spying on her and lurking in the shadows.

All she could do now was live her life, look after her children and animals. She needed to recover from her dreadful experience with Sicarus.

Fiona's recovery took a long time. Her scars had to heal, her mind had to heal. But they did, and never again would she become entangled with a bird. And she would help others to escape, too. Fiona and Maggie set up an advice centre in the temporary hut in the village to educate and help people struggling with relationships with birds. They planned to turn every temporary hut in every village into an advice and support group to help people dealing with birds.

Please be careful of the birds.